A MAGIC CIRCLE BOOK

SCHOOL ON A RAFT

written by **SARA SMITH BEATTIE**
illustrated by **GORDON LAITE**

THEODORE CLYMER
SENIOR AUTHOR, READING 360

GINN AND COMPANY
A XEROX COMPANY

Home Office, Boston, Massachusetts 02117

Far away on a jungle island were the villages of Binabo and Nepo. In the village of Binabo lived a boy named Half 'n' Half — he was half good and half bad.

Now Half 'n' Half had never gone to school and neither had any of the other children on the island because there was no school. They spent their days hunting and playing and swimming.

4

But the King of the island soon changed that. One day he decided that all small boys of the kingdom would go to school. The girls would remain at home to help their mothers. The King himself had been to school and he wanted the children of his villages to learn about the world.

5

One morning in Half 'n' Half's village, a huge gong was sounded and all the people came hurrying to the village circle. Standing near the gong was the village Wise Man. When he saw that all the people were seated on the ground, he spoke.

"Good people of our village, I bring you greetings and good news." The people smiled at each other. Even the children smiled, although they didn't know why.

"It is very good news," said the Wise Man, smiling as he looked at the small boys sitting in the dust. "The King has decided that we shall have a school."

"A school? What's that?" cried Half 'n' Half, forgetting that he was not supposed to speak.

"Quiet, boy," commanded the Wise Man. "It is only for grown-ups to ask questions."

"But, Wise Man," said an old man, "what is a school?"

6

The Wise Man turned and bowed to him, for he was the oldest man in the village. The elders were deeply respected. "A school, Old One, is a place where you go to learn about the world."

"Ah. But what do we need to know about the world? Is it not enough that we look after families and see to it that their bowls are filled with rice each day?"

"That is true, Honorable One, but there are still many more things to learn."

The Old One nodded his approval.

"Who will go to this school?" one father asked. "We do not have time for school. We have rice fields to look after and there is the fishing to be done. Who will do this if we go to school?"

"Ho, ho," laughed the Wise Man, "the school is not for fathers."

"Oh," said another father, "then who is it for?"

"It is for the young boys — Half 'n' Half, Toom Too, Pao, Ling Lee, and Chu. They will sit all day in the school and learn many things."

"For boys!" cried Half 'n' Half, jumping to his feet. "Why should boys go? I do not like sitting inside all day. I like climbing trees and swimming in the river. Let the girls go. Not the boys!"

The Wise Man was very angry. "Silence, boy," he thundered. "Twice you have interrupted. Off to the bushes with you and don't come back. This is grown-up talk."

8

Half 'n' Half stomped away quite cross. He
hated this school. No! He would not go. He
would not give up his play for that silly school.
Imagine sitting inside all day when he could be
swimming and playing. He knew all he wanted
to know. Half 'n' Half angrily kicked a bush.

9

After Half 'n' Half had been banished from the gathering, Wu Tang, father of Toom Too, inquired, "Where, O Wise Man, will the school be?"

"Well, the school will be on the river."

"On the river?"

The boys began to giggle, but one look from the Wise Man silenced them immediately.

"School will be held in a hut which will be built on a raft. It will be a raft-school."

"RAFT!" cried all the fathers. Everyone began talking at once.

"Patience, my friends," said the Wise Man. "I will explain. A raft-school will be most useful. On the first day of the week, the raft-school will float up the river. The teacher will teach the boys in the village, Nepo. The second day the raft-school will come down the river to our village. Our boys will go to school. On the third day the teacher will rest."

"So, our boys will go to school when the raft comes to Binabo," said Wu Tang.

10

"That is right," answered the Wise Man.

When the meeting was over, Toom Too, Pao, Ling Lee, and Chu went to look for their friend, Half 'n' Half. He was sitting in his favorite palm tree on the riverbank. They could see that he was in a very bad mood. His bad half was showing.

"Oh, Half 'n' Half, come down and play," they cried.

"I do not want to," he answered. "I want to think about this school."

"I think a raft-school will be fun," cried Toom Too.

"I do not think it will be fun," answered Half 'n' Half. "A raft, yes. But a school, no."

"But you will learn many things," said Ling Lee.

"I know many things already. I can dive deep in the river. I can slip up on the monkeys and pull their tails. Why, I even know where the turtles hide their eggs. And besides," he cried, angrily, "I do not want to sit inside all day."

Half 'n' Half jumped to the ground. "I might run away."

"Half 'n' Half, that is bad," cried Chu.

"I like being bad."

"But if you ran away, that would make your mother and father very sad."

Half 'n' Half cast his eyes downward.

12

"Why not try this school," continued Chu. "Then if you do not like it, you can run away."

Half 'n' Half nodded.

"Good," cried Pao. "I'll race you to the coconut grove."

"No," replied Half 'n' Half. "I am going for a swim."

13

Part II

Finally the morning came when the raft-school was to arrive. In some grass huts there was much excitement. Half 'n' Half's father gently shook his sleeping boy.

"Come, son, it is time for your bowl of hot rice. And since this is such a special day, you will have some fish with your rice."

"It is too early," yawned Half 'n' Half. "The sun has not risen."

"Today is very important. The raft-school will come."

"Oh, that. I am not sure I want to go."

"Quiet, boy. You do not know what you say. Come. You will go to school."

Half 'n' Half sat up and rubbed his sleepy eyes. He did not say more. He knew what he was going to do if he did not like the school. He ate the dish of steaming rice sprinkled with bits of dried fish. How good it was!

14

"And now," said his father, "you will take your dip in the river."

"I have a bright, clean loincloth for you," said his mother, smiling. Half 'n' Half took the loincloth, bowed to his mother, and dashed out of the hut.

Down the dusty path he ran to his favorite swimming place. He laid the clean loincloth on the damp grass, climbed high up on a large palm tree, and then plunged into the river. He came up gasping from the cool water.

"What fun," he thought as he tried to grab
a silvery fish.   Aloud he said, "I wish I could
stay here all day."

He could feel the sun's burning rays on his wet
back.   He climbed out of the river and wrapped
the loincloth around his waist.   Then he
tucked his homemade knife inside the loincloth
and headed for the hut.

As the sun rose high over the palms, a line of
fathers, mothers, and children headed for the
riverbank.   Everyone wanted to see the school.

16

At the river's edge, the people chatted excitedly.

"Is it not time?" asked one father, stretching his neck to see around the bend in the river.

"Patience, my friend," answered the Wise Man. "It will come."

"It comes! It comes!" cried an excited boy, swaying on a branch in the tallest palm tree. "The raft-school comes!"

"I can see it," came another cry.

"Move back," commanded the Wise Man. "I must get through. I must be there to greet the teacher." He pushed his way through the waiting crowd.

Around the bend in the muddy river came
a strange-looking raft.   It was made of bamboo
stems fastened together.   In the center was a
small grass hut with two holes for windows
and a hole for the door.   Near the hut stood
a short man pushing a bamboo pole again and
again into the water.   The raft floated up to
the bank.

"It is different from my raft," said Wu Tang.

"He must be the teacher," said another,
pointing to the man on the raft.

There was much talking.   Some people waved
palm branches.

The man tossed the anchor over the side, and
the water splashed onto the raft.   The raft
creaked and swayed for a few minutes,
then settled.   The man walked to the edge of
the raft, folded his arms across his chest,
and faced the people.

On the shore the Wise Man bowed low, then
spoke.

18

"Welcome to Binabo. I trust you are from the King."

The man on the raft returned the bow and then spoke. "Good people of Binabo, I bring greetings to your village from the King."

All the people bowed low. The man returned a deeper bow. Then he opened a long roll of paper. "I have a message from the King," he said. The people on the bank came closer. "I will read the message. It says —

A RAFT SCHOOL
IS HEREBY ESTABLISHED ON
THE RIVER TEEL. EVERY THIRD
DAY THE YOUNG BOYS IN
BINABO WILL ATTEND.
King Sun Cho Chow

"Our King is most kind," said the Wise Man. Then all the people bowed very low.

"I, Tay Yang, have been chosen honorable teacher," said the man. He gave a short bow. "We will not waste time. All boys will march into the school, please."

The boys looked at each other, afraid to move.

"Do not wait. We have wasted enough precious time. We will start at once."

Still the boys did not move.

The Wise Man called, "Come along. Step lively. You are wasting the teacher's time."

Each father grabbed his son's hand and started toward the raft.

"Oh, no," cried the teacher. "No fathers. Only boys. Fathers will go about their daily duties."

Each father gave his son a shove, and Half 'n' Half, Toom Too, Pao, Ling Lee, and Chu meekly marched onto the raft.

Inside the hut, the boys stood close together. "What will he have us do?" asked Chu.

"It's dark in here.   I can hardly see," whispered Half 'n' Half crossly.   "Are we to sit in the dark?"

"Maybe the teacher will let us sit outside," said Ling Lee.

Soon Mr. Yang entered.   "Sit down, boys." He pointed toward six small round bamboo seats and one large one arranged in a neat row.

At first the boys did not move, but the teacher insisted, "Take any seat."   The boys broke into a mad scramble, shoving and pushing each other for the biggest chair.

The surprised Mr. Yang looked around the room with dismay.   When the boys were finally seated, he said, "I see I shall have to make rules.   Yes, rules will be needed.   But for now there are more important things to be done." He then marched up to the front of the hut, stood with his arms crossed on his chest, and began to speak.

22

"Boys, you are off today on a new adventure.
One that you have never been on before —"

"Oink, oink."

"Today you will —"

"Oink, oink."

"What is that?   Who made that sound?"
cried the teacher.

23

"He did," cried Half 'n' Half, pointing to a fat pig digging at the sides of the hut.

"How did you get in here?" cried the teacher to the pig. A chorus of giggles came from the windows. Mr. Yang turned to see a row of heads looking in at him.

"Pigs and visitors are not allowed," said Mr. Yang. "Who owns this pig?"

"He is mine, sir," came a voice.

"Kindly remove him from the raft," said Mr. Yang.

A man shyly entered the hut and chased the fat pig around until he finally grabbed him.

"We-e-e," squealed the pig, as the man tucked him under his arm. Then he ran out of the hut, bowing to the teacher as he ran.

Mr. Yang stood at the door. "Friends," he said, "I can understand that you want to see what is going on, but this is not the way a school is run. We must not be disturbed. Kindly leave the raft."

24

The villagers scrambled off. With a yank on the wet grass rope, Mr. Yang hauled the anchor up. Slowly the raft began to float away from the bank and the teacher guided it with the long bamboo pole. The people were surprised to see the raft float away. So were the boys.

"Where is he taking us?" they whispered to each other.

"On a journey down the river perhaps," said Toom Too.

"Oh, joy!" cried Half 'n' Half. "I have always wanted to travel."

After a few minutes, the raft stopped drifting.

"Why, we are out in the middle of the river," cried Pao.

"Look," said Ling Lee. "I can see my father on shore. He is waving to me."

"Some journey," muttered Half 'n' Half angrily. "I hate this school even more."

"Quiet," warned Chu. "The teacher comes."

Mr. Yang returned to the boys, half smiling
and wiping his hands on his trousers. "Now we
shall get the peace and quiet we need.
Teaching school is hard enough without silly
interruptions.   There is much work to be done.
And we cannot spare a minute of this
precious time.   I will teach and you will learn."
The boys looked at each other.

"But first, we will get acquainted.   You there,
stand up," commanded the teacher.   The boy
obeyed.   "What is your name?"

"My name is Toom Too, sir."   The boy gave
a short bow.

"It is good to know you, Toom Too.   You
may be seated."

"Next boy," said the teacher.   "Stand up.
Your name, please?"

"My name is . . ." Half 'n' Half spoke
softly.

"Speak up, boy.   Do not be afraid to talk."

"It is Half 'n' Half, sir."

26

"Why would anyone call a nice boy
Half 'n' Half?"

"Oh, I will tell you.   Sometimes I am good
and sometimes I am bad, so I am half good
and half bad."   The other boys giggled.

The teacher looked at Half 'n' Half and said,
"We shall change the half that is bad."

"Oh, no," answered Half 'n' Half.   "I like
being the way I am."

"But surely you do not mean that. All boys want to be good."

"No. I like being bad sometimes. It is fun."

"Boys must not be bad. It causes trouble," replied the teacher, becoming annoyed. "You must change."

"No! No! No!" yelled Half 'n' Half. "I do not want to change."

"You will change," screamed the teacher.

28

"I will not!" he yelled again. He flew into
a rage and jumped up and down causing the raft
to sway.

The teacher angrily grabbed the bamboo pole.
Half 'n' Half dashed out of the hut with the
teacher right on his heels. Round and round
the raft they ran, screaming at each other.
Then, to the great surprise of Mr. Yang,
Half 'n' Half jumped into the river.

"Come back this instant," commanded the teacher, peering into the water. All he saw were air bubbles floating to the surface.

"You down there — come up here."

Half 'n' Half dived deeper and swam underneath the raft. He was furious. Suddenly he spied the grass rope that was tied to the raft's anchor.

"Ah ha!" he thought. "I'll get even with that teacher. Then I'll never have to go to school again."

Taking the knife from his loincloth, he swam quietly to the heavy grass rope and began cutting it near the anchor. Occasionally he rose to the surface for air, then returned to the rope.

One last big chop and the rope was cut. Half 'n' Half was very happy.

"Oh," he thought, "I must also get the bamboo pole." Silently he surfaced, tugged lightly on the pole, and sent it floating away in the water. "And now for a game of tag with the fish."

30

In and out he darted, under the raft and around the rope, scattering the fish as he went. The raft quietly drifted down the river. "This is far more fun than school," he thought.

Inside the hut, Mr. Yang was busy teaching the other boys. He no longer thought about Half 'n' Half, and he was unaware that the raft was drifting.

Half 'n' Half had good fun playing, but after a while he became hungry. "I will swim ashore and get some bananas," he thought.

As he swam for the riverbank, he heard
a very loud noise.   It sounded like thunder.
It couldn't be.   This was not the time of the
monsoon.   He looked up at the bright blue sky
and saw puffy white clouds.   "No," he
thought, "it is not a storm."   Then he
remembered — there was a waterfall down the
river.   He bobbed up and down to take a look.
The raft was headed toward the fork that led to
the waterfall!

32

As Half 'n' Half stared at the raft, he saw Mr. Yang rush out of the hut with Ling Lee, Pao, Chu, and Toom Too after him. Excitedly, the teacher ran around the raft searching for the long bamboo pole, the one Half 'n' Half had thrown into the water.

"Help! Help!" cried the boys.

"Half 'n' Half knew they were in great danger and he was responsible for it. He did not wish any harm to his friends, not even to the teacher. He must do something.

Half 'n' Half swam as he never had before. At last he pulled himself up on the riverbank and lay there panting. Never in his life had he felt so tired. Then he remembered the raft and seemed to gain back his strength. He scrambled to his feet and raced toward the waterfall, running through overhanging vines and branches, which scratched and tore his skin.

When he reached the falls, he took out his
knife and wildly cut into a long, strong vine
wrapped around a tree.

On came the raft, picking up speed as it
headed towards the waterfall.   It was not too
far from the riverbank, but the teacher and the
boys stood there helplessly, not daring to jump
into the swirling water.

"Just a few more seconds," thought
Half 'n' Half.   "I must be ready."   His hands
shook as he tied a rock onto the vine.

By this time Mr. Yang and the boys had
spotted Half 'n' Half.   They were not sure why
he was there or what he was up to.

34

Closer and closer to the falls came the raft.
Half 'n' Half stood ready to toss the vine
onto the raft.   It was still out of reach and its
bobbing motion made it difficult for Half 'n' Half
to judge his aim.   He flung the rock again and
again and each time the vine fell short of its
target.

Mr. Yang saw that it was useless.   "Come,
boys, let us go inside the hut."

"What will happen to us?" cried Chu.   "What
can we do?"

"Come," said the teacher calmly, and he
reached out a hand to the frightened boys.
They entered the hut.

Poor Half 'n' Half was sick with grief. He began to weep bitterly. He had done a terrible thing. "I cannot bear to look," he said and closed his eyes and waited for the crash.

After what seemed like a very long time, he slowly opened his eyes. "Oh Heaven be praised!" he exclaimed. For there, balanced on the edge of the falls, was the raft. It was caught on some rocks and the roots of some dead jungle trees. Half 'n' Half knew that he would have to work fast, because soon the roots would give way.

"Mr. Yang, Pao, Toom Too!" yelled Half 'n' Half. Slowly Mr. Yang stuck his head out of the hut. Then he saw what had happened.

"Come, boys," he commanded. "There is no time to lose."

Half 'n' Half swung the vine with all his might. Mr. Yang leaped up and caught it. Quickly he wound the vine through a window and out the door, then tied it tightly.

36

This made a crossing line from the riverbank
to the raft. The boys would have to climb
hand over hand on the vine across the water
to safety.

38

Mr. Yang gave the orders. "This is the only way you can save yourselves. Grab the vine and go. Remember, there's nothing below but the falls, so hang on."

"Yes, sir," said the boys bravely.

Up and over the falls they went. Mr. Yang came last and not a moment too soon. Just as his feet touched the ground, the straining tree roots gave way. The raft went over the falls with such force that the trees were snatched up and went twirling over the falls with the raft. The raft-school was shattered into a million pieces.

It was a few minutes before Mr. Yang and the boys recovered from the shock of their rescue.

"The village people will hear of your bravery, Half 'n' Half," exclaimed Mr. Yang.

"Yes, Half 'n' Half," shouted the boys. "You saved us!"

"Come, boys," said Mr. Yang, "we must get back to the village."

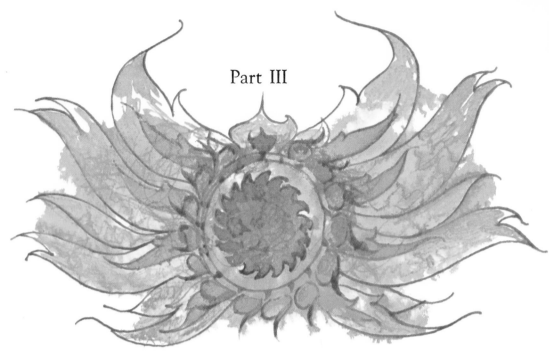

Part III

After a long walk in the hot sun, the boys and Mr. Yang arrived in the village.

The word soon spread about the runaway raft, and how the teacher and pupils were rescued by Half 'n' Half.

The Wise Man declared a celebration.   A feast was to be given to honor the hero.

Everyone was happy except Half 'n' Half.   He knew he did not deserve to be honored.   If he had not cut the rope in the first place, the raft would not have gone over the falls.

40

The gong sounded several times to let the people know it was time to start the celebration. Everyone sat down on palm branches to wait for the start.

Half 'n' Half was seated on a pillow in the center of the circle. To the right sat his parents and Mr. Yang. To the left were the Wise Man and the four boys.

The Wise Man stood. "Today we are here to honor a very brave boy — " At that moment Half 'n' Half tugged at the Wise Man's loincloth.

"O Wise Man, please may I speak?"

"Of course you may, boy. Speak as you wish."

"O Wise Man, honorable teacher, and parents — I do not deserve this honor."

"Of course you do," said Mr. Yang, interrupting. "Did you not save my life and the lives of your friends?"

"Yes, Half 'n' Half," said the boys. "You saved us from going over the falls."

"But you do not understand," cried Half 'n' Half.

"Perhaps you can help us understand," replied his mother.

"You see, I did not want to go to school. I wanted to travel. When Mr. Yang took the raft out on the river, I thought he was going to take us on a trip. But when he did not, I was angry —"

"But that has nothing to do with saving our lives," chanted the teacher and the boys.

"You do not understand!" wailed Half 'n' Half. "I cut the anchor which held the raft!"

"You what?" cried the villagers.

"You cannot mean what you say," moaned his father.

"Yes. Yes, I cut the anchor from the raft and threw the bamboo pole into the river. I am to blame. I did a terrible thing and I am very sorry." Half 'n' Half wept aloud.

"You are sorry!" bellowed the Wise Man, jumping to his feet. "Do you realize the seriousness of your deed? You must surely be punished."

"Oh, Half 'n' Half," said his weeping mother, "you have been a very bad boy indeed. I am truly ashamed of you."

"I know, Mother. I am ready to take my punishment."

"Good!" cried the angry Wise Man. "I am ready to give you your punishment. You have brought disgrace upon your parents and on our village. A whipping is too good for you."

"Just a minute, sir," said Mr. Yang, rising to his feet. "Did the boy not commit this deed at school?"

"Why, yes," replied the Wise Man.

"And am I not the teacher?"

"Of course you are, sir."

"Am I not the one to decide the punishment, since the boy was in my charge?"

"That is true," agreed the Wise Man.

"Then I will set the punishment. Half 'n' Half, you will step forward," commanded Mr. Yang.

Half 'n' Half, trying to look brave, stood before the teacher. Mr. Yang placed one hand on his shoulder.

44

"I want you to understand, son, that what
you did was very wicked." Half 'n' Half lowered
his head. "But it took courage to rescue us.
And it took greater courage to tell us that you
did a wrong when you could have very easily
kept it a secret. And now I shall have to decide
a punishment for you."

Mr. Yang stood thoughtfully for a minute,
then spoke. "You said you always wanted to
travel. Is that not true?"

"Yes, sir."

"Then travel you shall.   You shall travel
with me up and down the river aboard
the school-on-a-raft.   Your job will be to push
the bamboo pole and to see that the raft is
always in good condition.   You will study and
learn all you can in school.   You will work
hard.   Is that a fair punishment?"

At first Half 'n' Half could not speak.   He
was so surprised by the kindness of the teacher
that his mouth fell open.

"Oh, Mr. Yang," he cried. "I promise to learn everything. I will work hard. Never will the raft be in bad condition. I shall never cause trouble again. I promise. But we have no raft, sir."

"Oh, that is simple," replied Mr. Yang. "You and I will build another raft. But not now. I am quite hungry, so let's get the celebration started."

And the celebration began.

BCDEFGHIJK 765432
PRINTED IN THE UNITED STATES OF AMERICA